Binette Schroeder

Sir Lofty
& Sir Tubb

NorthSouth
New York / London

As everyone knows, in days of old, proud knights lived in mighty castles, fighting one another to pass the time. When they ran out of money, they sometimes "borrowed" from a passerby, who seldom complained. So it was with Sir Lofty and Sir Tubb.

Here they are now, our proud heroes: Sir Lofty and his gentle wife, Lucille, and his neighbor Sir Tubb and his beloved wife, Talullah. As you can see, the Loftys and the Tubbs get along surprisingly well—so well that they've let the old wall between their castles fall down. After all, what do you need with a wall when you hit it off?

Even when times changed, and the proud
castles grew a little crumbly, and the knights'
armor grew a little rusty, what did the Loftys
and the Tubbs care. They went right on visiting
each other, exchanging recipes and little
presents. After all, even if one is poor in money,
one can be rich in friendship.

Then one morning, Lady Lucille discovered something growing between two stones of the fallen wall. Beyond a doubt, it was something very special.

"This little plant absolutely needs fertilizer!" she cried, and she hurried to the compost pile.

Then along came Lady Talullah. "This little plant absolutely needs water!" she cried, and she raced for her watering can.

Even as they watched, the plant began to grow . . . and grow . . . and grow!

Sir Lofty and Sir Tubb interrupted their morning exercises and came running. The plant kept growing and growing and—"Aaaahhhh!" they all sighed—a large bud appeared.

Still the plant grew and grew and—"Ooooooh!" they all sighed—the bud opened to reveal twenty perfect petals.

Every morning, the blossom bowed softly to the east, toward the Loftys' castle. At noon, it stood straight upright in the midday sun. In the evening, it lowered its head gracefully toward the Tubbs' castle in the west.

Oh, what happiness there was! Each day, the Loftys and the Tubbs would meet under the flower. Each day, they would sing and eat and laugh and dance under the flower. That's how beautiful life was!

BUT (alas, there is *always* a BUT, and it usually means trouble) one night Lady Lucille could not sleep. She woke Sir Lofty.

"Actually, Loff," she said, "that flower is MINE. I discovered it FIRST. And every morning it is US it looks to. It is US it loves. It should ALWAYS look to us. Don't you think so?"

"Yes, indeed!" Sir Lofty agreed. Then he jumped out of bed and ran out the door.

"Don't forget the ladder!" Lady Lucille shouted after him. "And don't fall!"

Sir Lofty hurried down the stairs and out into the moonlit night. He tied one end of a long rope to the flower. The other end he tied firmly to his castle wall.

The next day, the Loftys, with enormous satisfaction, ate their breakfast, lunch, and dinner beneath the large blossom.

And what did the Tubbs have to say? "We don't talk to people like these!" And they slammed their castle door shut after them.

That night it was Lady Talullah who could not sleep. "The very nerve!" she cried. "If I had not watered it, that flower would NEVER have grown so tall! And it always ended each day with US. It's US it loves. It must ALWAYS look to our side! Don't you think so?"

"Absolutely," Sir Tubb agreed. Then he raced down the stairs and out into the moonlit night.

Sir Tubb tied the blossom to *his* castle wall. Then, with a satisfied smile, he went back to bed.

The next morning, insults flew
through the air like dragons.
"Gobble-snake!"
"Slime-belly growler!"
"Smelly-shelly sheepshank!"
"Stinky-finky pigger-wiggle!"
"Pigger-wiggle yourself, you
cockatoodle-beedle-doo!"
"I dare you to say that again,
you boggle-froggle!"
"Cockatoodle-beedle-doo!
Cockatoodle-beedle-doo!
Cockatoodle-beedle-doo!"
"That'll DO!"

Lofty grabbed.

Tubb pulled.

Lucille yanked.

Talullah tugged.

Then they all heard

a wailing **EEEEEEEEE!**

and the flower broke into pieces.

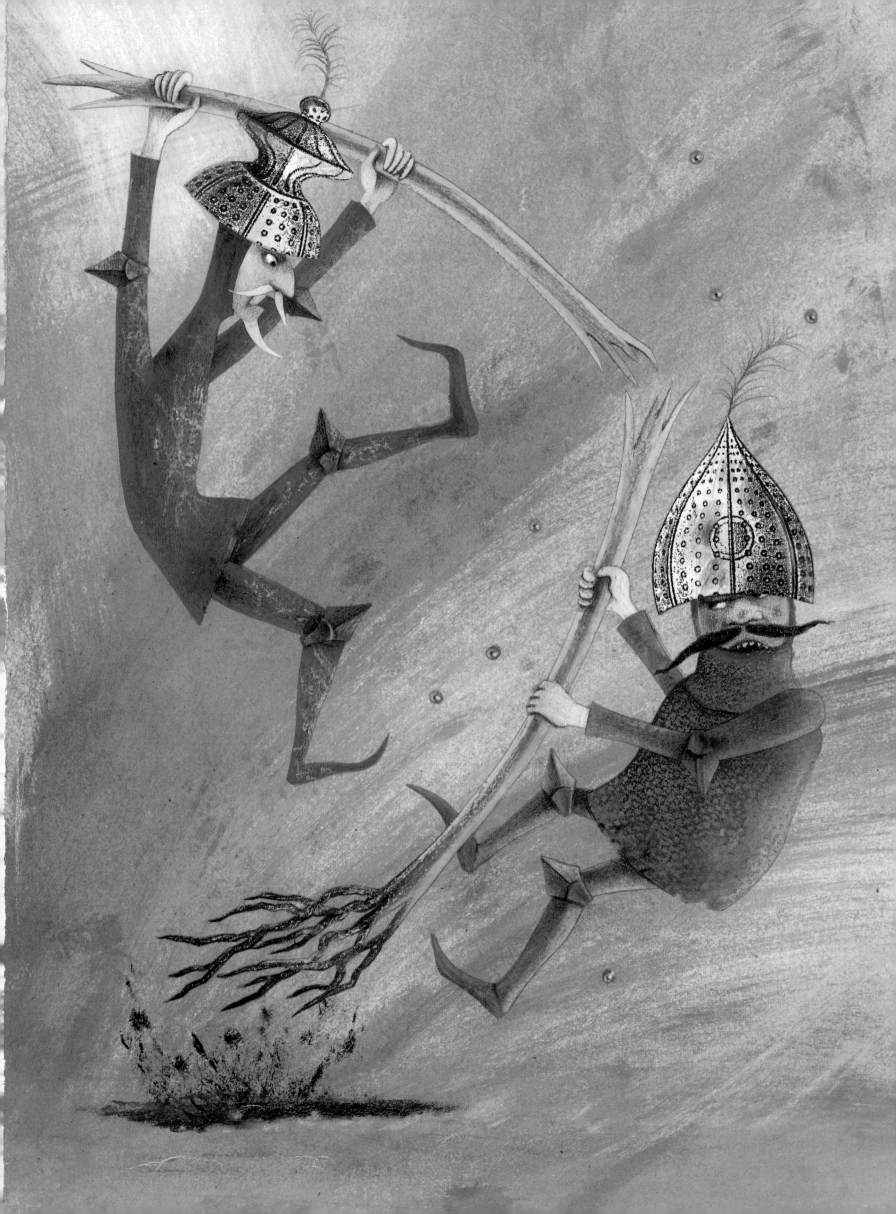

Before long, winter came.
It grew cold, both in the
garden and in the hearts
of the Loftys and Tubbs.
Between the castles there
grew a wall of ice.

BUT (there is *always* a BUT; and, fortunately, it sometimes brings good) after winter comes spring. And look how smart that flower was. Flowers aren't smart, you say? Who, then, scattered all the seeds in the gardens? Now there were flowers enough for all.

"We have seven!" counted the Loftys.

"So do we!" answered the Tubbs.

And they all rejoiced:
"How clever!"

The flowers listened.
And smiled.

First published in the United States, Great Britain, Canada, Australia, and New Zealand in 2009
by North-South Books Inc., an imprint of NordSüd Verlag AG, CH-8005 Zürich, Switzerland.
Distributed in the United States by North-South Books Inc., New York 10001.

Library of Congress Cataloging-in-Publication Data is available.
ISBN: 978-0-7358-2251-1 (trade edition).
10 9 8 7 6 5 4 3 2 1

Printed in Belgium

www.northsouth.com